AF373682

CROSS AND MISKATONIC UNIVERSITY

Duncan Blood's Journals

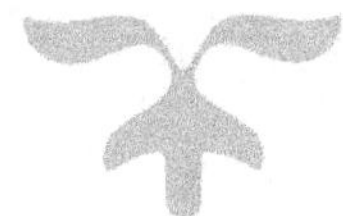

Nicholas E. Efstathiou

A Bit of History

The people at the Cross Branch of Miskatonic University have been a thorn in my side since the damned foundations of the school were laid. And in turn, I've laid more than a few of them to rest over the years.

Not all the bodies can be found, either.

Once more, some of my friends and associates at the Cross Historical Society have asked me to sit down and put pen to paper. One of them, George, has gone so far as to ask me to select some of the more, shall we say, interesting confrontations I've had with the faculty, staff, and student body of Miskatonic over the years.

And so, I've done as he asked.

There are few who will believe what is written on these pages, but that's fine with me. Believe or don't, it makes no nevermind as far as I'm concerned.

I'm finishing up another fine brandy sent to me from a friend up in Merrimack, New Hampshire. Good man. Family man.

More than I can say for myself.

Yes, I'm in a sour mood. Might be the brandy, although I suspect it's more from reflecting on the idiocies I've dealt with over the years.

You see, Miskatonic University is a bad place. The Cross branch is even worse than the main campus. There's a certain type of person drawn to Miskatonic, and I don't care much for that type of individual. Oh, there are a few who are good, but they're always the exception to the rule. Professor Moran was one such man, and I doubt there are many more I could name.

Part of the reason why I'm in such a state this evening is that there's been a spate of murders in town. Ritualistic killings. A reminder of what happened decades past when I found the corpse of the fat man hanging from my Gallows Tree. That, though, is neither here nor there.

No, tonight, I need to go to the university in town. There's been a bit more trouble up at the school, and soon I'll strap on the Colts and make that trip.

I've a feeling there's going to be gunplay tonight, and, I confess, it makes me smile.

Beginnings

It was a bad beginning.

In 1905, sick with cancer and close to death, Phil Jepson sold his lands to Miskatonic University.

I didn't please me.

I'd known of Miskatonic for some time, and I'd chased more than a few of their professors and researchers out of Cross in years past. The fact that they had managed to purchase land in my town was, to say the least, upsetting.

Cross has its secrets, and I've kept a great many of them for more years than I care to think about. The idea that some fool with a knack for ancient Greek was going to putter around my dead set my teeth on edge.

Shortly before Phil died, he told me that he had elicited a promise from the university. They were only to build a library on the lands, perhaps spread out to another building or two for research over the years.

I did not tell him that they had lied to him, for even as he lay on his bed, coughing up blood and bits of lung, they were breaking ground for far more than just a library.

The man with whom Phil Jepson had dealt was Judge Roy Cullen, a man whose family went back to some of the earliest settlers of Massachusetts Bay and Boston Towne. I'd killed a few of the man's relatives, and I had the suspicion that I might need to help him find his way to Hell as well.

When Phil breathed his last, I went out and found Judge Cullen standing near the excavated foundation. He was smoking a cigarette and admiring his conquest. When he saw me, the man gave a disdainful snort and then turned his attention back to the property.

I stood in silence, watching him, and after close to a minute, he turned around angrily, threatening to get the police to remove me from his property.

I walked past him, ignoring his continued verbal assault, and picked up a shovel.

Judge Cullen ordered me, of all people, to throw the shovel down.

Instead, I beat him with it.

As he lay gasping on the ground, his blood splattered across my face, I nodded, raised the shovel over my head and said, "Welcome to Cross, Judge."

The cracking of his skull was a pleasant sound in the cool evening air.

Trespassing

They have no sense of boundaries.

The University had built the library, and they were working on the next building when word came to me about the trespassers on my land.

According to the ghost who brought me the information, the University was constructing a chimney on one of the islands.

The fact that they were able to cross Blood Lake without being molested by any of the fell creatures in the water led me to believe that my damned mother had something to do with it.

I loaded my shotgun with birdshot, and with some extra rounds tucked into my pocket, I went out to Liar's Island, one of the smallest of them. It took a good hour to paddle out to it, and I was in no mood for foolishness when

I pulled the canoe up onto the island's only sandy spot. There was a larger, flat-bottomed boat as well and a well-worn path that stretched up and into the interior.

The sight of it set my teeth on edge, and I followed the trail of the interlopers.

When I arrived at the scene of the intrusion, I found a single man, one I recognized from the University.

His name was Bernard Laufey, and he was a professor who specialized in classical Greek. He was, according to the University library, there to approve or disapprove of volumes to include in the collection.

The man was standing not in front of a chimney but before a furnace.

I didn't bother asking him anything.

I pulled the trigger and shot him in the back of the legs.

He went down screaming, rolling over onto his side as I reloaded the weapon, the shell casings hot against my fingers.

Laufey stared at me in horror, and he struggled to face me.

I shook my head and aimed the weapon at him.

"Why?" I asked.

He pressed his lips together and refused to speak.

I shot him in the face, blinding him before I strode forward and dragged him by the hair to the open mouth of the furnace where fresh kindling had been laid.

As the man tried to escape, I took out my matches, set the kindling ablaze, and waited for the man to die.

It took a long time to happen.

The Siberian

He came to Cross to kill me.

In 1908, Doctor Marcus Ainsworth, president of the Cross Branch of Miskatonic University, decided that I was an unwelcome distraction. A roadblock, as it was, on the path to the school's bright future.

From what information I've since gathered, Dr. Ainsworth sought out and received permission from the board of directors to have me removed from Cross.

In order to achieve this rather remarkable goal, Dr. Ainsworth sent word to Europe, seeking assistance from an organization that helped Miskatonic obtain some of its more prized items. This group, whose name I have yet to unearth, agreed to the request and sent an assassin to eliminate me.

He arrived in Cross by way of train, traveling in from Boston. The assassin was met by Dr. Ainsworth in the train station, and the two of them retired to the school's campus.

By that evening, the assassin was in my house.

In a way, I felt bad for him. I don't believe Miskatonic warned him properly about me. Perhaps they didn't give him any information, or perhaps they only gave him what they felt was necessary.

Regardless of what was or wasn't said, the man was ill-prepared.

He came in through the back door sometime after ten. I'd turned down the lights and was sitting in the study, smoking my pipe and enjoying a glass of bourbon.

I had one of my Colts on my lap, and when I heard the whisper of a shoe across the ancient wood in the hall, I put down the bourbon and took up the pistol. When the assassin stepped into the room, I shot him in the belly.

The heavy slug tore through him, causing him to drop to his knees. As I turned up the light, I saw a look of surprise on his face. His hands were empty, but given the size of the man, I don't think he was planning on using a weapon.

He looked down at the wound, shook his head and then returned his gaze to me.

"Where are you from?" I asked.

"Siberia," he answered in Russian.

"Who sent you?"

He smiled and adjusted the green-tinted glasses he wore. "Ainsworth."

I nodded and blew his brains out.

One good turn deserves another.

Offices

They were worse than ticks.

By 1910, the University had the library, two halls and a pair of residences built on the land they'd acquired from Phil Jepson.

They had acres more they could use as well.

In the winter of 1910, they had finished a large office. Ostensibly, it was to be used for admissions into the school once it was fully up and running with a complement of students.

In reality, the damned thing was used to move items into Cross that had no damned business being there. Word came to me of a Hand of Glory that had arrived in August, a witch's hammer in September, and an actual scale of the Wyrm that had devoured a portion of Vesuvius in AD 79 and triggered the destruction of Pompeii.

The thought that these items, each powerful in and of itself, residing in any sort of capacity in Cross, displeased me.

I learned of them the hard way.

I happened to be in the post office when a package from Crete arrived. I was loitering at the window, talking with Del Watts, the postmaster, when one of the men voiced his wonder at where else the school was going to receive packages from.

Before anyone could answer his question, the package exploded.

The man holding it was vaporized, his remains painting the walls in a fine mist of organic matter.

I don't know what was in the package, and I don't care.

I helped clean up as best I could and then checked the loads on my Colts, loosened them in their holsters, and made my way to the University.

I went into the office and found a pair of men, neither of who were expecting me. They knew who I was, though, and before I could speak, they drew small revolvers.

I don't believe they expected me to draw my own guns, but I did. As their pistols barked in the confines of the office, at least one of the bullets striking me in the left arm, my Colts roared.

I admit I was irked, and I emptied all twelve chambers into them.

I left the bodies on the floor of the office and a message in blood on the desk.

"No more."

The school didn't listen.

Not at first.

Retribution

They misjudged her abilities.

Not that she wasn't skillful, mind you, she should never have been sent after me. Though I don't look it, I'm far too old for my head to be turned by a pretty woman.

Word about her arrival raced through town. She was both a stranger and attractive, either one of which would have made the proverbial grapevine burn with rumor.

I was out at Gods' Hollow when one of the Coffin boys told me there was a new woman in town and that she was interested in taking on work at one of the farms. He was on his way home to ask his father if they could hire her.

It doesn't take much to make me suspicious, and the arrival of this woman, less than a year after I had shot dead the two men in the office at the university, left a bad taste in my mouth. I didn't trust her, and so I went and settled into the woods across from the Hollow.

Within the hour, the woman was walking along the road.

Her eyes moved from left to right, and she kept to my side of North Road. Someone had warned her about the Hollow. The sound of a horse's hooves broke into the stillness, and the woman's demeanor changed.

Her pace slowed, a smile spread across her face, and she had the air of one relaxed and comfortable.

A moment later, old Jake Tepper came around the corner, and he slowed his horse down in order to tip his hat to her. I could hear them exchange pleasantries, and when he asked her where she was headed to, she replied that she was looking for Blood Farm.

Jake, being none the wiser, readily gave the woman directions to my home, tipped his hat again and went trotting off. When Jake was gone, she shed the guise of innocence and assumed once more the role of predator.

I didn't allow her to get much farther down the road.

I drew a Colt and put a bullet through her back.

The slug cut her spine in half, and she dropped like a sack of meal. As she lay gasping on the road, she tried to draw a pistol from her dress. Her hands wouldn't listen.

When she saw me, she snarled, hissing, "Blood."

I nodded.

"Someone will get you."

"No doubt," I told her. "But it won't be you."

The Orchard

He became tangled in the orchard.

It was October of 1923, and when I slept, I still heard the guns on the Western Front. On bad days, it was difficult to leave the house. I'd seen horrors before, but what I had experienced in France and Belgium was far beyond anything I'd witnessed prior to that war.

I awoke to a cold and bitter wind in my room, and when I opened my eyes, I saw my bedroom window was open. For a moment, a dryad loitered on the sill, a wicked look in her hard gray eyes.

"The Orchard, Blood," she told me, her voice reminiscent of dead leaves whispering across the earth. "Quickly, before he dies."

It's not often the fey are so bold as to come to my house, let alone open a window, so I took her at her word. I pulled on my clothes, slung my holsters and moved out a quick clip. Within a few minutes, I was at the apple orchard, and I could hear someone yelling.

I drew one of the Colts, pulled the hammer back and walked toward the cries, and soon I found him.

He was a large man, splayed out on his back and held in place by the thick and gnarled roots of a pair of apple trees. Close by was a bag which, upon examination, held all the accouterments of the professional arsonist. Leaving the bag where it lay, I turned my attention back to the prisoner.

Hunkering down near him, I holstered the Colt, found my pipe was still in my coat pocket, and I happily packed the briarwood bowl as the prisoner demanded that I help him.

With the tobacco smoking, I peered at him.

"Why are you here?" I asked.

"I'm lost," he answered.

"Seems like it," I agreed.

"Can you help?"

"I can."

He waited a moment, glared at me and then demanded, "Will you?"

"No," I said, shaking my head.

"What do you want?"

"Who sent you?" I asked him.

He eyed me, weighed his options and answered, "Miskatonic."

"To burn me out."

The man nodded.

I stood up.

"Are you going to let me go?" he asked.

"No."

"Why?!" he screamed.

"Because my trees like their meat fresh," I replied.

Before he could say another word, the roots tightened and pulled.

The sound of his limbs being torn from their sockets filled the orchard's silence.

Hubris

They don't know what they're dealing with.

For the last year or so, the fools at Miskatonic have let me be.

That's fine as far as I'm concerned. There are far too many other things for me to be concerned with. The Hollow has been more active of late, as evidenced by the foolhardy move upon the part of the university.

Jack Coffin stopped by this morning for coffee with a drop of whiskey. As we smoked our pipes, he mentioned he had seen a pair of new buildings in Gods' Hollow, just inside the border and where the stonewall ended.

The news of such an arrival is always of concern, so after we finished our coffee, Jack and I walked to where he had seen the buildings, and sure enough, they were still there.

One was a small house, and the other wasn't much more than a glorified shed, but their appearance was still a concern.

I considered whether or not to set them both on fire or to merely leave them be to see if the Hollow would send them along to some other place when elements of Miskatonic's staff arrived. There were several professors, a team of horses, and a half dozen men with a wagon full of equipment.

Neither Jack nor I felt compelled to interact with the newcomers, and instead, we watched them to see what they might do.

The stupidity was stunning.

Several of the men went into the Hollow, clearly uncomfortable with their task.

They went about their job quickly, and within a short time, they had the shed ready to move. As the men hastened out of the Hollow, another man, with an air of uncaring, strolled into the Hollow. He had a pipe held between his teeth, and he walked up to the horses, speaking to them in soft tones as he tried to soothe them.

It was of no use.

The shed came alive.

Multiple thin, wooden arms sprang out from the building's sides, dragging the man and the horses into the gaping mouth that the door had transformed into.

The screams of the man and horses were short-lived.

The monster that was the shed settled down, arms vanishing, mouth closing. Blood cooled into the snow, and those from Miskatonic fled the Hollow.

It's a pity more weren't eaten.

Magic

He was a practitioner of dark arts.
Professor Bert Hammar was a man skilled in magic. Not the magic of conjuring and illusion, rather he was proficient in spells both brutal and malicious.

He was, according to word at the university, scheduled to teach several classes regarding the translation of ancient magical texts. In actuality, I learned he was there to teach skilled students the finer points of creating and casting spells.

His first task, I was told, was to rid the university of an unpleasant thorn.

Me.

Hammar arrived on my porch late one evening, and weaponless, I answered the door. He asked to come in, and I obliged him, taking his coat and hanging it up before leading him to the study. As we sat down, I saw his nose twitch. The man could sense the magic in the house, and his eyes widened, then narrowed with greed.

I could see him calculating how best to search the house once I was dead.

He made small talk, to which I paid attention with half an ear, watching, instead, the way the fingers on his left hand moved. Clumsily they made arcane symbols, and I could see the mistakes he was making.

This was the wrong house to practice badly in.

He realized this a moment too late.

Hammar stiffened, tried to stand, and they were there.

I'm not quite sure what they are, only that they linger in the darker portions of the house. They are shadow and cold, nightmares trapped within the walls of my ancient homestead.

And Professor Hammar learned that the hard way.

They latched onto him and dragged him out of the chair. He opened his mouth to speak, though what he was going to say was lost as the shadows slammed his mouth closed and pressed his lips together. His wild eyes darted about the room, and they moved him inch by inch across the floor. There was a shadow, disturbingly large and deep by the hearth, and they were pulling him toward it.

When they reached the corner, they began to compress his flesh, blood exploding from his mouth and eyes, spurting from nostrils and ears. His body went into spasms, and a long, maroon smear was left on my floor as the nightmares vanished into the shadows of my house with their meal.

The Door

They're all fools.

The whispers came to me through the same shadows that Professor Hammar had been pulled through two years ago. Fell creatures told me of what the learned men at the university had done, and the information sent me out to the barn.

Something, goblins, I suspect, had disassembled the engine of the Ford I'd bought from Bill Coffin, and so I was forced to saddle up one of the horses.

It was later than I wanted by the time I reached the school, and I was forced to knock out the guard who tried to stop me from going onto the campus.

I hastened to the building where it was supposed to be, and there it was.

A Dead Door.

They were rare and brutal things. There was one on my farm, and I'd trapped my first love behind it because there was nothing else strong enough to hold her there.

This door was younger than mine but no less dangerous, and the damned fools had installed it into the side of a building.

Half a dozen of the professors were gathered around it in a semi-circle. Some were smoking cigarettes, and all were nodding and speaking in congratulatory tones. One man glanced at his pocket watch and stated, "He'll be out in two minutes."

Anger swept over me as I thought of the poor soul they'd sent through the door.

They chatted amongst themselves, ignorant of my presence, despite the annoyed snort of my horse.

As I swung myself out of the saddle, I pulled a Colt and slipped up behind the professors.

Still, they remained focused on the door.

"Ten seconds, gentlemen," the man with the pocket watch stated.

They went silent, and I braced myself.

The door was thrown wide, and a creature came screaming out.

It took me a split second to realize it was a man stripped of his skin, and I put a bullet through his head out of pure mercy.

Other creatures tried to follow, but my Colt roared, and they fell back.

I shoved the professors aside, grabbed hold of the doorknob and slammed the door closed.

The professors stood, horrified, staring down at the body.

"Set the damned door on fire," I snarled.

The sight of their volunteer dead on the ground hastened their steps.

Theft

Books are dangerous.

At times, this danger comes from the books themselves. This is evidenced by many of the volumes on my own shelves.

On other occasions, it is due to who owns the books.

Dr. Dawson Harmsworth, a librarian at Miskatonic University, learned this the hard way, which seems to be about the only way anyone at the Cross branch learns anything.

I'm still trying to piece out how he managed to get into my house. Or how he even learned of the book's existence. Eventually, when all is said and done, I'll know.

As it stands, he made his way into the house, into the first-floor library, and stole a copy of the Malleus Maleficarum. It is not the haunted edition that resides in my hidden library, but still, the book is rare in and of itself.

And he stole it.

I discovered the theft after dinner when I went into the library to sit and read. The book's absence was noticeable. The volumes had been rearranged around it as if to hide the book's removal. But I've been looking at my books for three hundred years, give or take, and I know where every damned one is supposed to be.

It took a hell of a lot of work to track the man back to the university but track him, I did.

I found him in the lower level of the school's library, my book in his damned thieving hands.

He attempted to scold me and force me out of the room, an act which would have been humorous had I been in a better mood.

I was not.

Instead of leaving, I locked the door to the lower level before I took my book from his hands.

The book is on a table now, and we're still in the school's library. Dr. Harmsworth's hands are on the table as well, as are both ears and one of his eyes.

He still hasn't told me what I want to know.

He will, though.

Still, I've paused long enough. I'll finish these notes when I'm home.

I promised I'd castrate him if he didn't tell me after I took out his eye, and I'm a man who keeps his promises.

Cats

They are not as sweet as they seem.

One of the night watchmen at the university found a pair of cats lounging on the stonewall that runs between North Road and the Hollow. Thinking the creatures lost, he called them to him, and they came. They followed him to the school and took up residence in the watchmen's quarters.

When I heard this, I went to speak with the president of the school. I told him, in no uncertain terms, that extending invitations to those from the Hollow was a poor decision.

He scoffed at my warning, told me that the salt of the earth needed their companions, and bid me good day.

I was about to go to the watchmen and pass my warning to them when a raven alighted upon my shoulder and informed me of a bit of trouble out on Blood Lake. The creatures under my protection are far more important to me than any at the school, and so I left to solve the problem on the water.

The issue proved to be nothing more serious than a pair of naiads who had drowned a trespasser from New Hampshire, and so after I disposed of his vehicle, I returned to the university.

It was too late for the watchmen.

When I walked up to the back door of the quarters, I found it open. I walked through an empty kitchen, down a narrow hallway and up to the second floor.

The cats were there, purring as they lay upon a desk blotter and peering at me with bored curiosity. On the floor around them were the skeletal remains of at least two of the watchmen. The yellowed bones, the ends broken open and the marrow missing, spoke volumes about the fate of the men who had taken in the Hollow's strays.

One of the cats licked its chops, and the other nodded to me.

"The house is ours, by right of conquest, Blood," it informed me.

"You'll get no argument from me," I replied.

The other cat paused in its cleaning and stated, "We thought not, but others of your kin have worried the matter to their regret."

I considered the statement and shrugged. "I'm not my kin."

Both felines chuckled, the dry, raspy sound following me as I left the house, closing the doors behind me.

Haunted

Some things ought not to be touched.

In May of this year, the scholars at the Cross Branch of Miskatonic University acquired a pistol for the school's museum. The weapon was a Colt, to be precise.

I learned of it this morning when I spoke with Dr. Martin van Burke, who had resigned from the school, told me that the Colt was purchased from a collector of haunted items. He had advised against the purchase, especially since there were rumors that the weapon had been responsible for the suicide of at least four previous owners.

Later in the evening, I reflected upon what the professor had told me.

I am no fan of the school, but neither am I pleased with the idea of such a weapon in the university's museum. Young men make poor decisions, and Miskatonic was full of such individuals, as evidenced by their choice in university.

I went to the school and persuaded one of the nightwatchmen to let me in. It was no great effort, not since I told him I'd knock his teeth down the back of his throat if he didn't.

With the man's coerced permission, I made my way to the museum and found the door unlocked and the lights on. Considering it was close to ten at night, I found this odd, and so I kept to the shadows as best I could.

I heard a pair of men arguing. One man's voice was thick and heavy, the other hollow.

A dead Federal soldier stood but a foot away from one of the professors, the living man holding the Colt in his shaking hands.

"You touched the damned thing," the dead man snarled. "Now you put the barrel in your mouth and pull the trigger!"

The professor groaned, tried to respond, but when he did, he unwillingly thrust the barrel of the weapon into his mouth and blew out the back of his skull.

I stepped forward as the body hit the floor, the pistol tumbling free of the now lifeless hand.

The dead man saw me, nodded and said, "You'll put me somewhere safe."

"I will," I told him. "With other ghosts, if you like."

The dead man considered the offer. "Aye. Like it, I would."

We left the fresh corpse behind us and spoke of war and suicide, things well familiar to us both.

Louise

She brokered no foolishness.

Louise Mathews had seen more than her share of heartache and pain in her 108 years of life. I'd known her for about 30 of those years, and when she had first made her way to Cross, I'd been worried for her. She took up residence in a small shack a little too close to the Hollow for my own comfort, but by the end of her first year, she'd managed to fight off several attacks by creatures that had gotten the better of folks half her age.

I didn't worry about her after that.

In the following decade, she worked odd jobs, scavenged what wood and materials she could, and built herself one hell of a house. I helped on occasion, but it was nothing more than hammering a few nails here and there. She didn't need any handouts, and I would have lost a good friend if I had tried.

Yesterday, a young man from Miskatonic attempted to drive her out of her home.

Part of it was because she's a black woman. Part of it's because she's old. Mostly, it's because they want her property.

Well, the young man was a fool.

She told him, in no uncertain terms, that she wasn't interested in selling her property. He told her he wasn't interested in buying it. She was going to gift it to the school.

That, according to Louise, is when I heard the gunshot.

Evidently, the young man didn't realize she had a scattergun pointed at him from underneath the afghan draped across her lap.

By the time I arrived, the young man was gone, though how he managed it, I don't know. There was a good deal of blood on the ground and where he had evidently parked his car.

Louise was still on her porch, reloading her scattergun and drinking rye whiskey. She grinned at me and welcomed me up. In her sweet, southern drawl, she told me what happened.

"He went back to the school?" I asked.

"It went back to the school," she answered.

I raised an eyebrow.

"Ain't nothin' of his manhood left, Duncan Blood," she informed me. "I hit what I aim at."

That she did.

Retribution

Things have a funny way of coming around.

I don't know that I'll ever get all of the story. Those that knew all of it are dead, all except one, and he wasn't in a mood to talk overly much when I saw him.

A short time ago, the rumbling of a steam engine on North Road caught my ear. It wasn't that steady, thrumming of a locomotive, but the odder, more peculiar sound of steam engine autos. I'd neither heard nor seen one in at least twenty years, so I confess my curiosity got the better of me.

The sound faded away, and I could tell it was headed into town.

I saddled one of the horses and followed after without any sense of urgency, although that would change by the time I reached town.

I'd no sooner gotten within a stone's throw of the library when I heard the heavy thud of a submachine gun. The noise came from the university, and I set my heels to the horse's side, sending the mare into a gallop.

The watchmen sprang out of the way, and I soon saw a curious-looking auto, the shape and design of which were utterly foreign to me.

Within a heartbeat, I was out of the saddle and moving towards an open door in the small building that housed the university's fledgling department of zoology. I had both Colts drawn when a trio of strangers emerged from the building.

Two of them were men.

The third was an ape of some sort.

One of the men, wearing a bowler hat, carried a Thompson submachine gun, a weapon with which he seemed terribly uncomfortable. The other man wore the uniform of a driver.

The ape was undeniably in charge.

He carried a swagger stick, and he wore a suit, his own soft cap worn jauntily upon his head. As the door was held open for him, the ape nodded to me.

"No need for those, Blood," he told me in a crisp British accent. "I've taken care of the bastards. They'll not come into my town again, that's for damn certain."

Without another word, he climbed into his vehicle, his man slipped in beside him, and the driver got in behind the wheel.

I holstered my Colts as they left, and then I did the same.

There was nothing more to do.

Experimentation

Curiosity killed them both.

There are some who would say it's a tragedy when anyone dies.

I'm not one of them.

Yes, there are some who should have lived longer than they did, just as there are some who live longer than they should.

Professors Small and Reynolds fell into the latter category.

On more than one occasion, I had chased both men from not only Gods' Hollow but from my property as well. The professors were chemists and had a propensity to trespass in order to obtain samples of chemicals and items which were not in abundant supply anywhere else.

From what I gathered, after their accident, they had amassed quite a bit.

Their foolish experimentation with their pilfered goods led to their timely demise.

There are a great many worlds and realities beyond our own. I avoid them whenever possible, and for the safety and sanity of others, I do advise the same.

I never bothered with the two chemists. I have learned that those at Miskatonic, for the most part, do not listen to anything close to reason.

Now, as the sun crested the horizon this morning, the men decided that the Ides of March was as fine a day as any to see what they might be able to do with some of their samples.

They succeeded in opening a door.

At 8:45 AM, a messenger from the school requested my assistance, and while I despise the people there, I cannot let their stupidity harm my town.

When I arrived at the school, I was escorted to the top floor of the Chemistry Building. I entered the main laboratory to find a scene of carnage.

Two piles of flesh and blood-soaked clothes lay in the center of the room. A door, no larger than a textbook, stood open. Several small men, dressed in tailored suits of bright blue and wearing neatly trimmed mustaches, smiled at me as they picked meat from their pointed teeth.

One belched, and his compatriots laughed good-naturedly.

Another of the men bowed and said in immaculate French, "Our apologies for the mess, Mr. Blood."

Before I could react, they closed the door and locked it shut behind them.

I shook my head and left the room. There was no need for them to apologize.

The mess wasn't mine to clean.

Unheeded

Some rooms are best left empty.

On Cain's Island near the southeastern shore of Blood Lake, there is a small house. It has stood for three hundred years come this autumn. It has been empty for the better part of two of those centuries, and the house prefers it that way.

I do what I can to keep the people away from my islands, but the pompous prigs at Miskatonic feel that the rules for others don't apply to themselves.

This morning, Cain's Island reminded them of the dangers inherent in my lands.

I was out on the shore, Colts loaded and scattergun in my hands, when I caught sight of a boat slipping around the lee side of the island. With some unpleasant words, I hurried to my dock and found one of my boats missing.

I was soon in a canoe and rowing hard toward Cain's Island. My mood was none too pleasant, and the darker creatures in the water wisely avoided me.

It wasn't long before I pulled in beside the rowboat someone had stolen from me.

There was only one path on the island, and it led straight to the house.

I disliked the building, and though I'd tried to burn it down on more than one occasion, it refused to stay burnt.

As I hurried up the path, I heard the voices of several young men and then that of an older man, and I bristled at the sound. When I stepped into the opening where the house stood, I saw them. Professor Briscoe and three of his students. The door to the house was closed, but the fact that the man and his students were facing it told me that they were waiting for someone to return.

I strode forward, and the intruders heard me.

One of the students tried to stop me, and I broke his jaw with the stock of the scattergun, dropping him to the ground.

Before anyone could speak, a high-pitched squeal issued from the house, and then there was silence.

The door swung open, revealing an empty room and an empty chair.

"Where's Jake?" one of the students whispered.

"Gone," I answered, cocking the scattergun. "Leave."

They picked up their injured fellow and carried him away, leaving me with the house. The door stood open a moment longer, and then it closed, its hunger sated.

Welsh

They invited him in.

I saw the Brening Tylwyth Teg strolling past the train station, and I nearly choked on my pipe. It's not often one sees the King of the Welsh fairy court, nor is it often that I want to.

He greeted me with a nod and a wink. In Welsh, he asked, "Will you walk with me, Duncan Blood?"

"That depends on where you're walking to," I replied in the same tongue.

The fey chuckled. "Oh, I do enjoy your company, Duncan. You're a damned sight more pleasant than your kith and kin."

"Most of them are dead," I replied, falling into step beside him.

"And by your hand," he said with another exaggerated wink.

"So, where are you walking to?" I asked. My hands itched to hold the Colts, but that would be only a false comfort. No weapon I had would do more than irk the creature beside me.

"To the university, of course," he laughed. "They've invited me in."

I blinked and shook my head.

"Oh," the king smiled, patting my arm. "I was almost as surprised as you. Word had come, as it does, of some serious inquiries upon their part. When I discovered they wanted to speak with me, in person no less, I was happy to make the trip."

I was still at a loss for words.

"Yes," the king's voice sank lower, darkness creeping into it and around his eyes. "I've asked to speak with their resident theologians, too."

"What of my town?" I inquired.

"Did you invite me in, Duncan Blood?"

"I wouldn't."

"Because you're not a fool," he remarked. "Your town is safe. I have words I wish to exchange with those who invited me. I will speak, and then I will leave. You should come back to Wales, though. Rumor has it that your mother has slipped in a few times. Or is it a few of your mothers have slipped in once?" The king shrugged. "I'm not certain. Will you join me at the school?"

"No," I answered. "I've a fear that you might get a little too excited."

He let out a deep laugh, nodding his head enthusiastically. "That I might!"

He gave me another pat on my arm, and we separated.

Five members of the faculty vanished from a locked room that night, and they've not been heard from since.

No

It was masterful and elegant.

The grand hall of the Cross branch of Miskatonic University was everything one would expect to find in a school dedicated to higher education and to hidden decadence of thought.

I'm not quite sure how much money was spent on the building's construction, though there were whispers that it was upwards of a million dollars, perhaps more. I know that special wood had been harvested deep in the Teutoburg Forest in Germany, and the crystals in the chandeliers were rumored to have been crafted in vile homes in Paris.

The building, known as Miskatonic Hall, was the gem of the school.

When it was finally finished after three years of continuous work, the building was an absolute masterpiece. I confess that when I looked upon it for the first time, I was impressed. The architect, from the same firm that had designed the chapel at the United States Military Academy at West Point, had outdone himself. As I walked through it, I could see the sigils and symbols hidden in the wood and the floors. When I listened, I heard the whisper of the creatures hiding within the walls and lurking in the subfloors.

Yes, it was everything that the school hoped it would be, and after my initial visit, they did not allow me near the structure.

I don't blame them.

The university and I are not on amicable terms.

True, they did invite me to view the structure, but it was more to flaunt what they had accomplished than to solicit my opinion.

I was impressed that they put additional guards at the front gate, and they even set up a system of roving patrols.

This morning, as I was drinking my coffee and considering which apple trees needed a fresh feeding, my house was shaken by an explosion. When I reached town, I went and stood with the rest to look at the ruins of Miskatonic Hall.

The staff members were beside themselves with anguish. Their first faculty soiree was to have been this evening.

I confess that I felt bad when I saw the smoldering ruins.

I was never any good with explosives. The finer points of timers always seem to elude me.

Dinner

The dinner wasn't quite what they were expecting.

The university was still reeling from the destruction of Miskatonic Hall, but they decided to hold their gala event nonetheless the following weekend. I made it a point to secure an invitation for myself, though they were loathed to present me with one. I was forced to remove several teeth from the president's mouth before he relented.

I had some words I wished to share with the faculty, staff, and some visiting dignitaries about staying off my lands and out of the Hollow.

I found myself a seat by the door, and I refused to eat or drink. I was quite content to smoke my pipe and bide my time. After the appetizers were finished and the second and third bottles of wine were opened at the tables, I figured it was high time I spoke to those gathered.

Before I could, Professor Malcolm Cummings stood up at the head table. He swept a hand over his bald head, adjusted his black bow tie, and invited those gathered to enjoy the fine, exquisite freshwater squid pulled from Blood Lake.

His words chilled me to my bones, and I knew there was no use in speaking.

Dinner would speak for itself.

The servers brought out silver bowls, each one holding a small, roasted squid.

Or what they believed had been squid.

I knew better.

There were no freshwater squid in my lake, though some of the Elder Gods had been known to spawn in the depths.

As the first of the guests dug into their meal, I stood up and walked to the door.

Someone called my name, their tone high and imperious, and when I turned back, I merely shook my head. A few of the professors laughed, but only for a heartbeat.

For those who had begun to eat, well, they began to burn.

Blue flames, the color of sapphire, burst from every orifice, searing and devouring flesh.

As the flames jumped from body to body, I closed the door behind me and made my way home.

My own dinner was waiting, and I was famished.

Trouble

He should have stayed in the Hollow.

It's been almost two years since the members of Miskatonic discovered their mistake regarding the freshwater squid they pulled from Blood Lake.

I've heard nary a peep from the school, and I've been quite happy about that.

Unfortunately, it seems that the institution has been nursing its wounds and plotting some sort of revenge. No, not against the denizens of the lake.

Against me.

And it seems that those in charge of the school have sought to solicit help from the Hollow in my removal.

One of my ravens intercepted a messenger, a carrier pigeon of all things, and brought the information home to me. I've the small scroll on the desk in front of me.

"Your offer of payment is acceptable to my mistress," an unknown hand has written. "She would like nothing more than to see this version of her son dead."

Always pleasant to know that my mother is still alive in one form or another, although I confess I'm somewhat disappointed in the staff at the school. While I didn't believe any of them had much in the department of common sense, I thought they were at least smart enough not to make deals with the likes of my mother.

Well, that's neither here nor there, I suppose.

According to the rest of the scroll, someone from the school is to meet their hired assassin at the stonewall.

I combed my hair, trimmed my beard, and put on my funeral suit. I resisted the urge to strap on my Colts, and instead, I tucked my Bowie knife into the small of my back. It was uncomfortable as hell, but it was necessary.

By the time I reached the wall, I'd worked up a fine sweat, and I was feeling a trifle piqued when I caught sight of the man. He was sitting against a log, eating his lunch. He paused long enough to ask if I was from the university, and I said I was.

He nodded, took another bite of his sandwich, and was still chewing when I drew my knife and drove it through his chest.

It took but a minute's hard work to sever the head, and I carried it with me into town. I left it in the center of the school's entrance, surprise on the dead man's face.

I hope their expressions mirror his own.

The Researcher

Some questions should not be asked.
Professor Reginald McFee joined the Department of Science at the Cross Branch of Miskatonic University in

1929. He was a man exceptionally skilled in the fine and delicate art of chemistry. He was focused, dedicated, and extremely reluctant to speak of his work.

On a July night, I found out why.

There had been a rash of disappearances over the past two months, and I was doing my damnedest to find where the missing people were.

All told, there were seven people, adults and children, missing. Not a single clue could be found, which was damned unusual for Cross. On most occasions, I can pick up something, and I had decided to resort to calling in a few favors when I spotted something unusual.

A man was hurrying along the road towards the University, and over his back, he had a large gunnysack. From it came a mewling noise, similar to that of a cat in distress.

Since the man was not headed toward the veterinarian's office, I followed.

His path took him to the science building on the campus, and I entered the building a moment after he did. The man's well-heeled shoes rang out on the stairs and hid the sound of my own soft treads. When I reached the second floor, I caught sight of the gunnysack as it disappeared into a laboratory on the right.

I was halfway to the door when I heard a wail, and I knew it was the cry of a child and not an animal.

I was too late to save it.

When I eased the door open, I saw Professor McFee standing over a sink while a noxious cloud with a greenish cast to it rose toward the ceiling. The professor shook his head and muttered, a sound that stopped when I drew my Colt and cocked the hammer back.

Startled, the man turned around, his eyes wide and his belly heaving.

When I asked him where the child was, he gestured toward the sink and explained that the child, like the others, had failed to prove his theory that a soul could be captured.

I put three slugs into his belly, and as he lay dying on the floor, I told him I was testing a theory of my own.

If I'm right, I'll see him in Hell.

December 24, 1938

The echo of my Colts rolled across Gods' Hollow's open field and reverberated off the tree-line.

I had spent most of the day in pursuit of a creature whose origins were unknown to me. I had tracked it from the Cross Branch of Miskatonic University, where it, and several of the students, had feasted on the body of a young man from Athol. The students were easy enough to kill, the creature, whose shape shifted as it ran, proved to be more challenging.

Finally, exhausted and ready for the day to be finished, I walked up to the still writhing beast and gazed down upon it. Bluish-black blood melted the snow and sent tendrils of a noxious vapor into the air. From its tongue came an undulation that was an undeniable plea for mercy, and it was a plea which I ignored. I put a pair of rounds into its head and was pleased to see it die.

As I extracted the empty shells and reloaded the chambers, I heard a curious sound from off to my right, and as I turned and looked, I confess myself surprised.

Of all the strange and wondrous sights I have been witness to, never before have I seen Father Christmas on a sled being pulled by a pair of turkeys.

The birds moved at a decent clip, and as I holstered my pistols, Father Christmas waved his hand to me and bid me a good day in fine and proper German. I returned his greeting and watched as he and his team disappeared into the tree-line.

Christmas in Cross was always an event.

December 25, 1940

I tracked him from Cross to New London, Connecticut.

His name was Albert Franks, and he was a professor of ancient languages at the Cross Branch of Miskatonic University. It was he who had brought forth the creature I had killed two years earlier on Christmas Eve, and it was he who had lured the young man from Athol. Professor Franks had done so with the promise of work, for the young man had been destitute and hoping to provide for his mother and younger siblings.

When I found Albert, he was sitting in his mother's home, sitting between two of his sisters. Because of the revelry going on, none of them had heard me enter. For several minutes I stood in the kitchen, listening to them talk. Albert, it seemed, shared all his ideas and hopes with his family, and they, in turn, supported him fully. I listened with growing disgust as he elaborated on his plans to gather up several more sacrificial victims to see if he could open up a door within the school to one of the other worlds. When I heard his mother suggest some of the 'street urchins' who could be found on the wharf, I decided I had listened to enough.

I stepped into the room with my pistols drawn, and all looked upon me with surprise. While his siblings and mother argued that they had nothing to steal, Professor Franks understood who I was and why I was there.

To his credit, the man did not run, nor did he beg.

He was horrified, though, when I gunned down his family around him, the guns roaring in the confines of the room. As their blood and brains splattered him, he sat immobilized, too shocked to react.

And that was fine.

A single round through his forehead ended the hunt, and a bit of turkey quieted my hunger for the ride home to Cross.

Weakness

I have returned home to war.

I've been in the Pacific for a bit of time, fighting the Japanese and, if I'm to be honest with myself, enjoying my time immensely. Oh, I've drifted home every so often, checking on the town and my lands. Making sure nothing has gotten too out of hand.

I've returned to what I thought was peace and quiet, but I should have known better.

I expected a bit of the same – nonsense from the Hollow and perhaps one or two incursions by those in charge of Miskatonic University. What I did not expect, however, was the all-out assault on my person.

The men who sit on the board of directors at the university know me too well, I'm afraid. They know that I am far older than I seem and that I am, by my nature, bound to protect this place.

And so they set a trap for me.

One that nearly succeeded. Had they used fire instead of an explosive, they might certainly have ended me.

Instead, they made me angry.

They have gone from being a nuisance to something that needs to be eradicated.

It was the fey who told me about the trapped child in the abandoned house on Coffin Road. They didn't know there was anything wrong with the place. Why would they? They are unfamiliar with explosives.

I made all haste to the building, and when I drew near to it, I heard the voice of a child. The fear in the child's voice was not feigned, nor was it a recording.

I did not think the house was a trap.

I did not think those at Miskatonic would use a child as bait.

But they did.

When I opened the door and stepped into the building, I saw the hole into which the child had fallen, heard its pleas, and when I moved in swiftly, I triggered the device.

I was wounded, painfully so, but what is far worse is that the child was killed.

It took me several hours to crawl out from beneath the rubble. Hours in which I heard the board members of Miskatonic congratulate themselves on the removal of my person.

In the morning, I'm going to hunt them down, one by one, and punish them.

Oh, what they've got coming.

One

I will teach them the meaning of fear.

Ten men sit on the board of directors for the Cross branch of Miskatonic University.

I will kill them from last to first.

Doctor Alfonse Smyth is a saw-bones, a man who got away with murder while operating on POWs during the Great War. When he came back to America, he was well-suited to set up shop as a butcher in a private hospital just outside of Boston.

I know how he established himself in the university's system and how he climbed and clawed his way onto the board of directors.

He provided victims for whatever brutal experiments the main campus thought necessary to engage in.

His mistake was coming to Cross and raising his hand against me.

He is the newest member of the board and thus the least among equals.

I find him in the sumptuous apartments he keeps in one of the buildings on campus. One they believe I don't know about.

But there's little I'm unaware of.

Especially now.

The fey have been my ears, the ravens my eyes.

My hands will speak for me.

Standing outside the main door to his apartment, I can hear Smyth chatting with someone on the phone. Within ten minutes, his conversation is finished, and I hear him moving around.

The lock opens at a touch, and I slip inside.

I can hear the water running in the bathroom, and a moment later, I see him. He is naked, his flesh a sickly white.

I am unarmed, for my hatred and my hands are all the weapons I need.

In the space of a heartbeat, I am in the bathroom, stuffing a towel into his throat and gouging out his right eye as I drive him into the tub. It shakes on its clawed feet, and water splashes across my boots. I jerk out the towel, and as he gasps for breath, preparing to scream, I thrust his eye into his mouth and force him to swallow it.

When he realizes what he's just eaten, Smyth faints, but hot water in his empty eye socket shocks him back to consciousness. When he tries to scream, I clamp my hand over his mouth and shake my head.

"We'll have all night for that," I tell him, and he faints again.

Smiling, I thrust my thumb into the empty socket and help him wake up.

Two

Neat and orderly.

Doctor Chas Leith lived off-campus in a small, tidy home. He had been a widower for the better part of twenty years, and after he retired from teaching geology at the main campus, he had taken a position on the board in Cross.

It was a poor decision on his part.

When the sun crested the horizon, I followed Dr. Leith from his home to a small office in the Department of

Natural Sciences. It was, I knew, his one stipulation for taking the position on the board and moving to Cross. He needed a place to call his own outside of his home and on school grounds.

I appreciated this caveat.

It made the task easier.

Dr. Leith was far too preoccupied with his own thoughts to notice me, and I was not making any great effort to remain hidden from him. He even went so far as to hold the door open for me as I entered the building behind him.

He was only truly surprised when I stepped into his office.

The good doctor opened his mouth to ask me a question, but a sharp strike to his larynx silenced him and sent him staggering back to his desk. I caught him by his tie as his glasses went clattering across the floor, and I slammed him down into his chair. As he tried to escape my grasp, I drove his letter opener through his right hand, pinning it to the arm of his chair, and then I used his scissors to secure his right in the same fashion.

That freed his voice, and he managed a solitary shriek before I shoved the phone's handset into his mouth, breaking teeth as I bound it in place with the cord.

I closed the window and drew the blinds, ensuring that we had some semblance of privacy before anyone became aware of my presence on the grounds. Soon enough, they would find Dr. Smyth's remains, and it wouldn't take them long to figure out who had done it and why.

I had to make the most of the situation.

Picking up Dr. Leith's pipe, I filled it with some of his tobacco, lit it, and enjoyed a pleasant smoke as I let the enormity of his predicament settle over him.

Smiling, I drew my pen knife, opened it up, and went about the long and tedious process of removing his face.

Three

There is no mercy in my heart.
Not for these men.
They knew what it was they were doing. Oh, I'm not terribly upset with the attack on my person. That, at this point in my life, is merely par for the course.
It's the death of the child.

The death of Doctor Wallace Lewis' grandchild, to be precise.

He had offered the boy up as a sacrifice.

This morning, having enjoyed a breakfast and a cup of coffee at the Cross Diner, I heard one of the waitresses remark that her son's playmate, Joshua Lewis, had been sent to live with relations in Georgia. I found this to be curious. I know, for a fact, that Dr. Lewis and the boy were the last of the line. Lewis' son and daughter-in-law had died in an auto crash during the war, and there were no other family members to speak of.

None that Dr. Lewis would have sent the boy to.

I entered Lewis' house shortly after noon and found the man sitting in a chair beside a chest of drawers with a photo of his grandson atop it.

If that was meant to move me to pity, it failed.

When Lewis saw the knife in my hand, he sneered and said, "I gave the boy up for your death. You could have had the common courtesy to die."

The southern drawl he spoke with was abrasive and reminded me of the men I had killed during the War of the Rebellion.

"I could of," I told him, stepping forward.

He tried to draw a small revolver, but I sprang forward and knocked it aside. As he attempted to bring the weapon to bear, I drove my weapon down, the blade of the Bowie knife castrating him.

His squeal of pain echoed off the high ceiling, and the revolver clattered to the floor. The man's eyes were wide as he clawed at my hand, trying to get me to pull the blade out.

I twisted it instead.

Leaving him pinned to the chair, I tore open his shirt and began to break his ribs one by one.

He lived for a long and terrible time.

Four

He had a winning smile.

Doctor Lyle Fisher was a man who prided himself on his ability to win over even the most hesitant of investors when it came to the university. Whether it was a natural talent or one he cultivated, there was no denying his charisma. He had a near immaculate set of teeth, the charms of an aristocrat, and the skills of a diplomat.

I'm certain he expected to talk his way out of death whenever it came for him.

Alas, I am not death.

I'm a Blood, and I deal in death. Pain, when it's called for.

And right now, it's called for.

I could hear Fisher on his phone, murmuring soft words of reassurance. He was, from what I gathered, telling one of his colleagues that there was nothing to fear. That the other three members of the board had been struck low by some foul creature unleashed from the Hollow, and nothing more.

The idea that something from the Hollow was considered less of a threat than myself brought a smile to my face.

But the smile didn't last long.

A moment later, Fisher hung up the phone, and I heard the telltale rattling of glasses.

I was surprised to find the door unlocked, and by the expression on his face, I could tell he was surprised he had forgotten to secure it.

In one of his hands was a large decanter of brandy. The stopper for it was in the other, and while he could easily have thrown them both at me to buy himself some time, he did not. Instead, he stood frozen in place with fear.

A heartbeat later, he soiled himself, and I was in the room, closing the door behind me.

He tried to speak, but the words were nonsensical.

He didn't fight as I took the decanter and the stopper away, nor did he struggle when I forced him into his chair.

In a matter of moments, he was bound to the furniture, his terror-filled eyes never leaving me. I drew my Bowie knife and his eyes fixed upon its tip.

As I squeezed his mouth open, Fisher understood what was about to happen, and he howled as I used the weapon to dig out the first of his teeth.

With a flick of my wrist, I sent the tooth clattering to the floor, and I whistled while I worked.

Five

He thought he was something special.

Professor Elliot Ravensworth was of the opinion that he and he alone could handle matters relating to the Hollow. How he came by such a bloated sense of self-worth, I'll never know.

Not that the lack of information will keep me up at night.

There's little that does.

Regardless of his abilities, I will admit that he was prepared when I entered his home.

He just wasn't prepared for me.

I've been shot plenty of times, and while I don't enjoy the experience, it hasn't ever kept me from doing what needs to be done.

When I stepped through the back door, he shot me twice in the chest and once in the stomach with a .32. There wasn't enough of a punch to the bullets to do much more than cause me to pause, and I grinned at him, nudging the door closed with the heel of my boot.

"Now, Elliot," I said, drawing one of my Colts, "that's mighty impolite."

He tried to squeeze off another shot, but I pulled the trigger, the slug of the Colt tearing through his forearm and causing him to drop the .32 to the floor, his hand hanging useless. When he tried to stagger back toward the hall, I put a bullet into his gut while the one in my own body was pushed out the hole it had made.

The impact of the Colt's .44 caused him to slump against the wall and then sink down to the floor. His face took on a deathly pallor I was well-familiar with and one that – at this moment in time – irritated the hell out of me.

I cocked the Colt's hammer back and aimed the weapon at his right knee.

"You've got a choice, Elliot," I told him. "A quick death or a slow one."

"What do you want?" he whispered, blood staining his lips.

"Who planned the attack?"

Elliot hesitated, and I put a bullet in his knee.

He screamed and then shouted, "Killingly!"

Hank Killingly, the head of the board. First among equals.

"End it," Elliot whispered.

"I will," I told him.

"No," he shook his head. "Me."

"I already have, Elliot. You'll bleed out soon enough."

I sat down in a kitchen chair and smiled, his weak curses music to my ears.

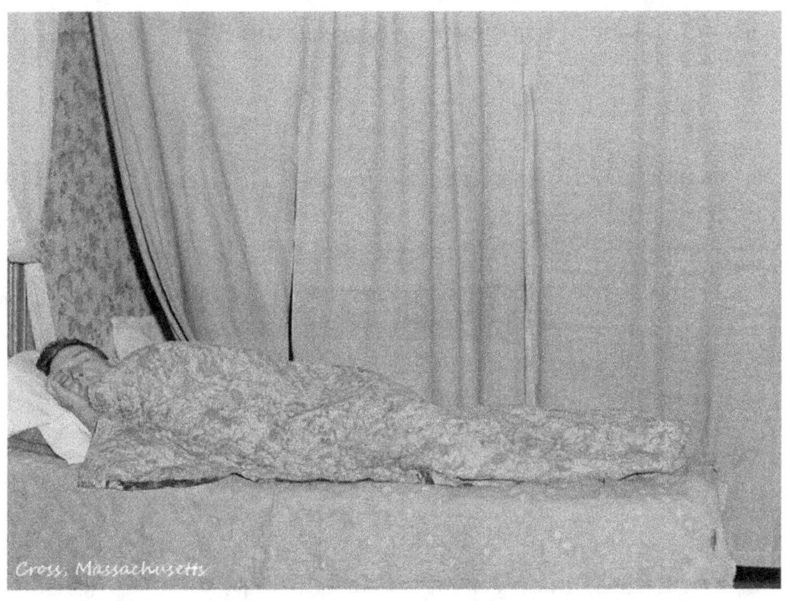

Six

The man's death was frustrating.

It took me the better part of a day and a half to find Doctor Stephen Kahn, who was next on my list of men to kill.

Unfortunately, he denied me that pleasure.

Several members of the fey court tried to assist me with locating the man, but he'd taken precautions against such an action. Kahn may have been a bastard, but he knew he was going to die, and he wanted to slow me down as much as possible.

There is a bit of grudging admiration, I'll admit, but I didn't feel that at the time.

I eventually located him in the basement of the local chapter of the Red Cross, the members of which were off in Boston for a week-long training. How Kahn had finagled the keys from them, I'll never know, because I don't want to listen to the Red Cross folks complain about the sanctity of their building.

No place is safe.

Not when I'm angry.

And I was furious when I located Kahn and found him dead by his own hand. He took poison, and he must have taken one I'm not familiar with. More than likely, it came from the Hollow, and I wonder at how he knew of its efficacy.

He looked as though he were asleep, and had it not been for the rank and foul stench of death in the room, I would have believed him to be.

But Dr. Kahn was dead, and he had escaped my good justice.

He could still be useful, though. If he had told his companions of his plans, or if he had kept them to himself, he would illustrate a point.

I dragged his body out of the basement, and in the spacious backyard of the Red Cross' property, I butchered him. I worked for two hours, making sure each piece was prepared the way I wanted, and then I brought him to the university. When the nightwatchmen saw me approaching in my truck, they wisely retreated to the safety of their guardroom.

In silence, I parked the truck, got out, and arranged the severed limbs and innards of Kahn in the driveway's entrance. The last piece was Kahn's head, and I made certain it was facing toward the main building.

On his forehead, I had carved a single word into his pale flesh.

"Soon."

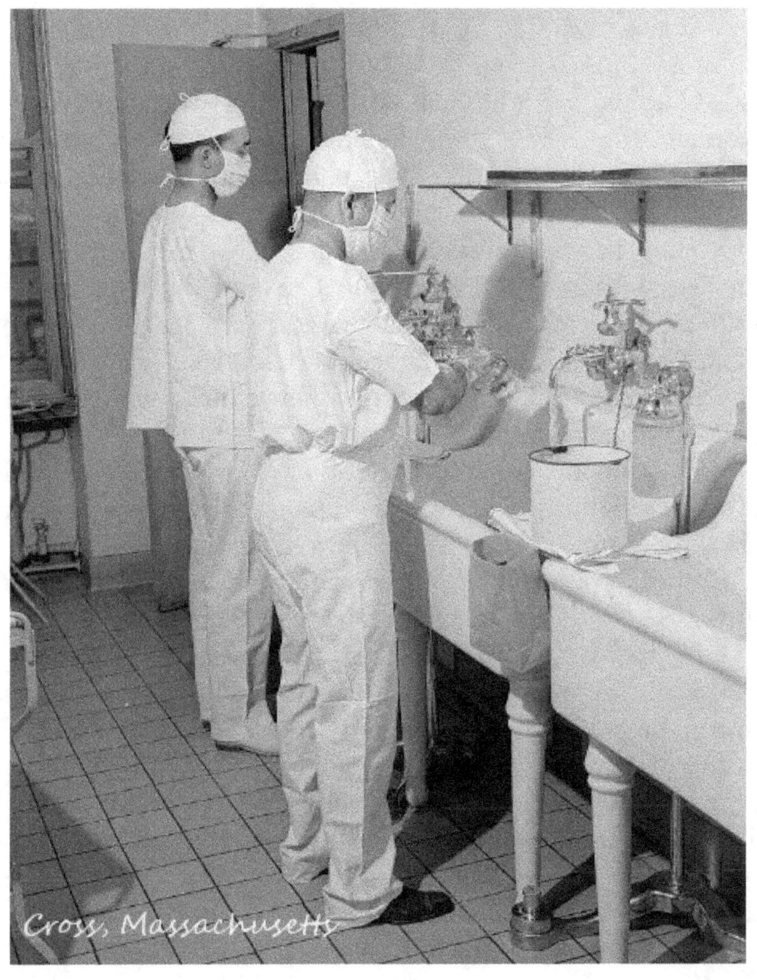

Seven and Eight

It was an abomination disguised as a surgery.

In the depths of the university's newest building was an operating theater that rivaled any on the East Coast. The finest pieces of equipment for the most delicate of surgeries could be found within its gleaming walls, and those who operated there did so under the pretense of goodwill.

Doctors Ronan and Christian Hope were monsters masquerading as men.

Oh, they were human, born much the way any man or woman might be. Their hideousness was a product of upbringing and wealth. Their parents had spared the rod and spoiled the children and the men that they became.

They had achieved their status as board members of the Cross branch of Miskatonic University by way of the foul experiments they conducted and wrote about. I knew of the men, and they had earned their place on my list of chores long before the murder of their colleague's grandson and the attempt on my life.

I've no idea as to what surgery they were preparing themselves for, but I caught both men unawares. They were chatting, lost in conversation and excitement when I entered the room. Their nurses were dead in the other room, throats slit. A quieter death than any of them deserved.

Neither of the Hope brothers would escape their fate.

I put the muzzle of a Colt behind Christian's ear, and in a matter of moments, he had secured his brother to one of the operating tables. Then, under my watchful eye, I had him wheel out a second table, and then I bound him to that. The men peppered me with questions as I set about the task of cutting off their clothes, and as fear gripped them, they demanded answers.

Silence is an effective tool.

Soon, their voices had risen several octaves, their eyes darting to the doors, as though they were expecting someone to come and rescue them.

They should have known better.

I learned of torture at the hands of masters. Hurons and Iroquois, who administered and withstood levels of pain most would find unbearable.

With those memories at hand, I took up a scalpel from a tray of surgical tools.

I confess the sharpness of those blades impressed me.

Nine

He hid his fear well.

Doctor Peter Stockham, originally of New York City, came to a stop just outside the entrance of the Department of Languages. Despite the calm smile on his face, the hand on the door-latch betrayed his nerves.

There was nowhere for him to run.

No safety he might find. Neither inside the building nor outside of it.

And he knew it.

"Duncan," he said, clearing his throat, his smile broadening.

I nodded.

"Would you care to walk with me?" he asked.

I shook my head. "Let's go inside."

His face paled. "Well, you know, I really can't. Not right now. There's a bit of work that needs to be done, and I'm to meet with the Hope brothers for dinner."

I smiled. "They've had to cancel, I'm afraid."

Peter's Adam's apple bobbed nervously, and his grip on the door-latch tightened. His eyes darted from left to right, and I said softly, "Best not to try and run."

"Would you shoot me down?" he asked, eyes fixing on the Colts on my hips.

"As easy as I draw breath, Peter," I replied. "But it won't be to kill."

His eyes widened, horror spreading over his features.

"Why?" he whispered. "What have I done?"

"You helped to kill the boy."

"That was Hank Killingly's idea!" Peter hissed. "I only wanted to get rid of you."

"But you went with it," I reminded him.

The man took a step forward, releasing the door-latch and fumbling in his overcoat. I waited until he drew the pistol he'd hidden within it, and I drew down on him.

The Colts roared, slugs tearing through his thighs and sending him spinning backward. Blood was smeared across the old doors, and despite being knocked down, Peter didn't lose his grip on the pistol in his own hand.

With a howl, he rolled onto his stomach and pulled the trigger, his body shuddering once.

Disgusted, I flipped him onto his back and saw the coward had shot himself in the heart.

I considered mutilating the body for a moment, but then I decided against it.

My anger was stoked and hot.
It was time to deal with Hank Killingly.

Ten

Hank Killingly had lived longer than he should have.

I found him on his property, the old professor humming to himself and seemingly oblivious to the world around him. This, I knew, was all an act.

Of the many things the old bastard was, oblivious was not one of them.

I did not hide my approach as he stood with his back to me, examining the beauty of the sky.

"Have you come to kill me, Mr. Blood?" he inquired.

"In a manner of speaking." I spat my words at him, and I was pleased to see his back stiffen.

My anger was evidenced in every syllable I spoke.

He turned around, revealing the sawed-off shotgun in his hands. Both barrels of the weapon were pointed at my stomach, and I raised an eyebrow. He smiled.

"You're a tad more difficult to kill than I first imagined, Mr. Blood," he informed me. "But I've no doubt that a belly full of shot will put you down long enough for me to find a way."

"Hank, you pull those triggers, and you're going to die in the worst way I can imagine."

He smiled and shot me.

He pulled the triggers.

The shot tore through my stomach and shredded my innards. I took a step back, glaring at him, but I didn't fall.

I didn't even lose my balance.

His look of utter surprise was worth every ounce of pain.

He tried to break the weapon open and reload it, but shock and growing terror caused him to fumble the weapon and drop it. As my stomach struggled to knit itself back together, I moved forward, ignoring the shrieking agony of each step, and struck the man with an open palm.

Hank babbled and begged as I shoved him back against a broad pine tree, and his hands clawed at me as I took hold of them and jerked them backward. By the time my belly was done with its repairs, I had him tied to the tree and naked.

"I learned this in Afghanistan," I told him, drawing my knife. "And it takes a damned steady hand."

I made the first incision at his breastbone and whispered, "You shouldn't have killed the boy, Hank."

In the stillness of the afternoon, Hank Killingly screamed as I skinned him alive.

Quarantine

It was designed as a quarantine facility, not by anyone from the state of Massachusetts, but by several professors of the Cross Branch of Miskatonic University. I was against the construction of the building, but my opinion didn't carry any weight on that particular matter.

Over the years, various creatures were accidentally – so I was told – summoned by various professors and their adjuncts. These creatures and some people directly affected by them were housed in what was euphemistically known as the Recovery House.

No one, and nothing, that went into the building recovered. To enter it was a death sentence. Invariably, the people died. The creatures, well, some of them died peacefully, others I later discovered, died from experimentation.

Evidently, the learned men believed that the creatures lacked any rights, seeing as how they were not of this world.

I disagreed.

I tried all the rational, reasonable channels first. And I was turned away each time. Politely, but still turned away.

One evening I went to the Recovery House to speak with the staff, to see if I could not convince someone there to allow me in. I sought to at least send the creatures back from whence they came.

No one allowed me entrance.

As I stood on the stoop, arguing with the night watchman, I heard screaming. It was the high-pitched cry of something being tortured and tortured for no reason.

I killed the night watchman where he stood and moved indoors.

The House was a nightmare, and I killed far more people and unknown entities than I wanted to. There was no saving any of them. The creatures were near death, their tormentors unworthy of life.

When I finished, there was nothing left living in Recovery House. When I went to the university, I left none of the offending professors alive.

~

I'd like to say that I don't hate the Cross branch of Miskatonic University, but that'd be a lie.

I do hate it.

There are few good things that come forth from the university, and those that do, well, they're more the exception than the rule. I've put down a great many men, a few women, and scores of creatures I've no names for that have come out of the school. I suspect that I'll put down more long before Death comes and reaps me.

I could be wrong, of course, but something tells me that I'm not.

The reapers have told me that I've a gift for killing, and there's no denying it. I've lived a long time, and at the rate I'm going, I don't believe I'll be dying any time soon.

There are too many that need killing.

Far too many.

Duncan Blood
4/21/2021